Maths Together

There's a lot more to maths than numbers and sums;
it's an important language which helps us describe, explore and
explain the world we live in. So the earlier children develop
an appreciation and understanding of maths, the better.

We use maths all the time – when we shop or travel from one
place to another, for example. Even when we fill the kettle we are
estimating and judging quantities. Many games and puzzles
involve maths. So too do stories and poems, often
in an imaginative and interesting way.

Maths Together is a collection of high-quality picture
books designed to introduce children, simply and enjoyably, to basic
mathematical ideas – from counting and measuring to pattern and
probability. By listening to the stories and rhymes, talking about
them and asking questions, children will gain the confidence
to try out the mathematical ideas for themselves – an
important step in their numeracy development.

You don't have to be a mathematician to help your child
learn maths. Just as by reading aloud you play a vital role in their
literacy development, so by sharing the *Maths Together* books
with your child, you will play an important part in developing their
understanding of mathematics. To help you, each book has detailed
notes at the back, explaining the mathematical ideas that it
introduces, with suggestions for further related activities.

With *Maths Together*, you can count on doing the
very best for your child.

For Robert

First published 1994 by Walker Books Ltd
87 Vauxhall Walk, London SE11 5HJ

This edition published 1999

2 4 6 8 10 9 7 5 3 1

© 1994 Nick Sharratt
Introductory and concluding notes © 1999 Jeannie Billington and Grace Cook

This book has been typeset in Frutiger Roman.

Printed in Singapore

British Library Cataloguing in Publication Data
A catalogue record for this book is
available from the British Library.

ISBN 0-7445-6830-7 (hb)
ISBN 0-7445-6804-8 (pb)

My Mum and Dad Make Me Laugh

Nick Sharratt

WALKER BOOKS

AND SUBSIDIARIES

LONDON • BOSTON • SYDNEY

My mum and dad make me laugh.

One likes spots and the other likes stripes.

My mum likes spots in winter

and spots in summer.

My dad likes stripes on weekdays

and stripes at weekends.

Last weekend we went to the safari park.
My mum put on her spottiest dress and earrings,
and my dad put on his stripiest suit and tie.

I put on my grey top and trousers.
"You do like funny clothes!"
said my mum and dad.

We set off in the car and on the way we
stopped for something to eat. My mum had a
spotty pizza and my dad had a stripy ice-cream.

I had a bun.
"You do like funny food!"
said my mum and dad.

When we got to the safari park it was very exciting. My mum liked the big cats best.

"Those are splendid spots," she said.
"And I should know!"

My dad liked the zebras best.

"Those are super stripes," he said.
"And I should know!"

But the animals I liked best didn't have spots and didn't have stripes. They were big and grey and eating their tea.

"Those are really good elephants," I said.

"And I should know!"

About this book

Reading *My Mum and Dad Make Me Laugh*
together is an ideal way for your child to begin
to notice and understand pattern and describe
what they see. There are many kinds of patterns
in the book using spots and stripes. These include
different colour combinations, sizes and shapes.

Though few mathematical words are used
in the story, the clear illustrations provide
many opportunities for you and your child to
recognize, notice and compare patterns together.
This is an essential part of mathematical thinking.
Young children respond to visual aspects of shape
and pattern. Later on they use this knowledge
to learn more about the patterns and rules of
numbers as well as shapes.

Notes for parents

Looking together through the pictures, your child can point out everything which has spots and stripes. They could start by looking at Mum or Dad's clothes.

What's Mum wearing now?

Spotty slippers, a spotty jumper, a spotty skirt...

The zebra crossing's got fat stripes.

You can encourage your child to talk about the patterns and describe them in their own words. Don't worry if they don't use quite the "right" words – they'll soon learn to say *thick* or *wide* instead of *fat*.

The stripes on his shirt go from side to side.

Yes, and the ones on his trousers go up and down.

By comparing the patterns on each page, your child will begin to notice all sorts of similarities and differences.

Children can have fun copying some of the patterns in the book or making up their own designs.

They can also make a "double picture" by painting on one side of a piece of paper, folding it in half, pressing hard, and then opening it out to see the design.

Pattern words

Dominoes and other matching games like Snap and Pairs help your child to look for, and recognize, patterns.

Patterns are all around. Look for them on trees, food packets, clothes – at home, in the park, or at the shops.

Maths Together

The *Maths Together* programme is divided into two sets – yellow (age 3+) and green (age 5+). There are six books in each set, helping children learn maths through story, rhyme, games and puzzles.

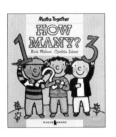
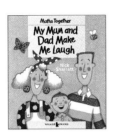

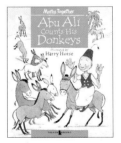